Enid Blyton's

MAGICAL TALES

Bumble and
the Elves

and other stories

W0006887

This is a Parragon Book

© Parragon 1997

13-17 Avonbridge Trading Estate,
Atlantic Road, Avonmouth, Bristol
Produced by The Templar Company plc,
Pippbrook Mill, London Road, Dorking,
Surrey RH4 1JE

Text copyright © Enid Blyton Ltd 1926-29

These stories were first published in Sunny Stories,
Teacher's Treasury, Two Years in the Infant School,
Read to Us, New Friends and Old and
The Daily Mail Annual.

Enid Blyton's signature mark is a registered
trademark of Enid Blyton Limited.

Edited by Caroline Repchuk and Dugald Steer

Designed by Mark Kingsley-Monks

Printed and bound in Italy

ISBN 0 7525 1711 2 (Hardback)
ISBN 0 7525 2326 0 (Paperback)

Enid Blyton's

MAGICAL TALES

Bumble and the Elves

and other stories

PARRAGON

Contents

Bumble and the Elves

MR Bumble was having some painting and whitewashing done in his cottage. Mrs Bumble had said that really the walls were getting dreadfully dirty, and the ceilings weren't fit to be seen, so Bumble had said he would have the house all nicely painted, with some lovely new wallpaper in the parlour.

"I'll get the painter elves in to do the walls and ceilings of every room except the parlour," he said. "I don't think they would be much good at papering. I shall do the papering!"

Mrs Bumble looked at Bumble, and wrinkled her rosy face.

"Oh, Bumble," she said, "do you think you ought to? You know you're not very good at doing things for the house. Don't you remember when you tried to paint the shed? You lost the paint five times, couldn't find your brush, and ended up by stepping into the paint-pot and spoiling your new shoes."

"Fiddlesticks!" said Bumble crossly. "This is a very different sort of job. I shall be most careful. All I need is a roll of pretty wallpaper, a pot of good paste, and a paste-brush. I don't think I can get into much trouble with *that*, can I?"

The next week the painter elves came in to start painting the house. They were a lively lot and Bumble didn't like them very much because they were not very polite to him. They wanted to tell him the best way to paper the parlour, too, and he didn't want any help from anyone.

The very first day he started on his work he made a bad mistake. He didn't look carefully enough at the paper he was putting on the wall, and when one of the elves peeped in to see how he was getting on, how he laughed!

"Oh, Mr Bumble!" he cried. "You've gone and put that piece

on upside down!"

And so Bumble had! He stared at it angrily and then tore it off. "I'm sure I had it the right way up when I measured it on the wall," he growled to himself. "Perhaps one of those cheeky little elves popped in and put it the wrong way up for me. I shouldn't be a bit surprised."

The next day the elves peeped in again, and found Mr Bumble in great trouble. He could *not* seem to make the paper stick on the wall. It fell off as fast as he pasted it on. The elves looked at his paste-pot and then laughed heartily.

"Oh dear, oh dear, that Mr Bumble's a funny old man!" they giggled. "He's trying to paste his paper on the wall with Mrs Bumble's furniture polish!"

Bumble looked down at his pot – and to his surprise and disgust he saw that he *had* been using the polish-pot instead of the paste-pot! No wonder the paper wouldn't stick to the wall! The paste-pot was standing in the corner where he had put it the day before.

Bumble was very angry when he heard the elves laughing. He shook his brush at them and told them to go away.

"Back to your work!" he cried. "I believe it was one of you who played this trick on me, putting the pot of polish for me to use, instead of my paste-pot! Yes, you're a set of tiresome nuisances! Be off to your work in the next room!"

The elves went, looking rather scared. Bumble certainly had a bad temper!

Now the next day Bumble worked very hard indeed – so hard that after a little while he needed a rest. So he put his paste-brush down on a chair – which he certainly shouldn't have done, for it made a mess – sat down in another chair and closed his eyes for a little nap.

Whilst he was gently snoring, Mrs Bumble came in to ask him what he would like to have for his supper that night. When she saw Bumble was asleep, she smiled, and sat down patiently on a chair to wait for him to wake up. She took out her knitting and began to knit.

Now, although she didn't know it, she had sat down on the very sticky paste-brush! Mrs Bumble was fat, and wore very wide, full skirts, and she had no idea at all that she was sitting on the paste-brush. She sat there, knitting quietly – and then someone came to the back door. Up got Mrs Bumble and went to see who it was, the paste-brush sticking to her skirt. She let the parlour door bang and that woke up Bumble with a jump.

"Dear, dear!" he said, opening his eyes and yawning. "I've been to sleep. This will never do! I must get on with my work!"

He looked for his paste-brush and it wasn't there! Then how angry he was! "It's those tiresome little elves !" he cried. "They've slipped in here whilst I was asleep and taken my brush!"

He rushed into the next room.

"Where's my brush?" he cried to the startled elves. "Come, don't look so surprised! I know you've taken it. Give it to me at once or I'll punish you!"

"We certainly haven't got your brush," said the elves, and no matter what Bumble said, they stuck to that. They had *not* got his brush.

"Very well," said Bumble, looking very fierce. "I shall now put a spell on whoever has it. That will teach you a lesson, you mischievous creatures!"

He waved his hands in the air. "May whoever has the brush be punished by it!" he cried. "May

he be slapped in the face by it!
May he be pushed on the nose by
it! May he be pasted from head
to foot!"

He stopped and glared at the
elves, to see which one would be
punished – and at that very
moment there came dreadful
shrieks from the kitchen, where
poor Mrs Bumble was making a
cake. The paste-brush had
suddenly jumped up, and was
slapping her on the face, and
covering her with paste! She
pushed it away with her hands,
but it came back again and again,
till she was sticky from head to
foot. She rushed into the room

where Bumble and the elves
stood listening in surprise to her
screams, and called out to
Bumble:

"Look at your paste-brush!
Make it stop, make it stop!"

Bumble stared in horror. Then
he said a few magic words and
the brush hopped peacefully into
its pot where it stayed.

And then, what a bad time
Bumble had, explaining to Mrs
Bumble what had happened!
How angry she was! How she
scolded poor Bumble!

"I must have sat on your nasty
brush when I came into the
parlour for a few minutes," she

said. "What do you want to leave a paste-brush on a chair for, you silly creature? That's the end of your paper hanging, Bumble! Go to the bedroom and tidy all your drawers and cupboards. That will keep you out of mischief. Elves, you can paper the parlour as soon as you've finished your other work!"

Poor Mr Bumble! He *was* glad when all the work was finished, for you have no idea how those elves chuckled and laughed whenever they saw Bumble creeping quietly about the house! He *did* feel ashamed of himself!

Away Went the Panda!

WHEN James went out to tea he took his panda. It was a beauty. It was white with big black rings round its eyes, and it grunted when James squeezed its tummy.

"James simply *loves* Panda," his mother told Mrs Hill. "He'll enjoy showing it to Jane. He's very, very proud of Panda."

James didn't very much want to show Panda to Jane. He was afraid she might want to play with him. He didn't like anyone else playing with his toys, and especially not with Panda. He stood and stared at Mrs Hill, hoping that she would say that

Jane had a panda, too. If she had, she wouldn't want to play with his.

"What a beauty!" said Mrs Hill, trying to take the panda. James held on to it. Mrs Hill laughed. "Don't you want me to hold him, James? Well, I won't then. Jane! Where are you? James has come to tea with his new panda!"

"Oh, James – how lovely!" said Jane when she came downstairs. "I haven't got a panda. I've got three dolls and two teddies, a clockwork mouse and a monkey – but nobody has ever given me a panda. Does he growl?"

"He grunts," said James, and pressed the panda in the middle.

"Oooof!" said Panda at once, and Jane gave a squeal.

"Let *me* press his tummy, James! Let *me*!"

But James wouldn't. Nobody was going to have his panda except himself. Nobody would press his tummy. Jane mustn't even hold him!

As soon as Jane saw that James wasn't going to let her play with Panda, she began to tease him. She ran after him. She tried to snatch Panda. She tried to punch him in the middle to make him grunt. James soon became very angry indeed.

How he wished he hadn't brought Panda! He usually liked Jane, but he didn't like her at all that afternoon. He clutched Panda fiercely and turned his back on Jane.

"I shall tell Mummy you won't let me play with your Panda," said Jane at last, and ran out of the room to find her mother. James stamped his foot. What a tell-tale Jane was! Now he would have to give her Panda, and be told off too.

"I'll hide him!" he thought. "Yes, that's what I'll do. I'll hide him somewhere." He darted into a nearby bedroom. He saw a basket there and so he popped Panda into it, shutting down the lid tightly.

Jane soon came back. "I can't find Mummy," she said, sulkily. "But I'll tell her about you, when she comes in. What have you done with Panda? You haven't got him now. Where have you hidden him?"

James didn't say anything. He went to the toy cupboard and took out a box of bricks. He began to build a house.

Jane ran all over the place, trying to find Panda. Then she got tired of it and went over to

James. "You aren't building that house right," she said. "Look, you have to put the windows in like *this*!"

Soon they had forgotten their quarrel and while James built the house, Jane made a garden for it, building a little fence, and setting up little tubs of toy flowers and trees. It all looked very nice.

Nobody said any more about Panda at all. He wasn't mentioned till it was time to go home. Then, when James was putting on his hat and coat, he suddenly remembered Panda.

"Panda!" he said. "I must go and get him."

"I'll get him," said Mrs Hill. "Where is he?"

"Er – well – I put him in a basket in a room next to the playroom," said James.

"Whatever for?" asked Mummy.

James didn't answer. Mrs Hill went upstairs to the bedroom. She looked in her sewing basket, but there was no panda, only her sewing things.

"It isn't there, James," she said, when she came back. "You can't have put Panda into the basket. Now do think where you put him because Mummy is waiting to go home with you."

"I *did* put him in there," said James, and he ran up the stairs to the bedroom where he had hidden Panda. There was a green basket in a corner of the room – but that wasn't the basket he had put Panda in. That had been a big one, with a big flat lid. It had been standing on the floor near the wardrobe. He told Mrs Hill.

"Oh, *that* basket!" said Mrs Hill. "Why, that was the laundry basket, you silly boy – and the laundry man came this afternoon, and took it away. It was full of dirty clothes! Oh, James – he must have taken Panda, too!"

James looked horrified. "Will he – will Panda be washed and put through the wringer and hung up to dry? Oh, Mrs Hill, he'll be so miserable."

Jane burst into tears. "You shouldn't have hidden poor Panda away," she wailed. "Mummy, he's a horrid, mean boy. He wouldn't let me play with Panda, and he hid him away – and now the laundry man's taken him, and Panda will be boiled with soapy clothes, and squeezed in the wringer till he's all flat and horrid, and..."

James looked as if he was going to start wailing, too.

Mummy took him firmly by the hand and led him away home.

"You were unkind to Jane, and now you've been unkind to Panda," she said. "How many more times do I have to tell you that you must share your toys and your sweets and everything with other people? Now because you wouldn't share Panda, you've lost him altogether."

Poor James! It is a dreadful thing to lose a toy you love, but it's even worse when you lie in bed and imagine him with soap in his nice black eyes, and boiling water all round him – and then the wringer squeezing him flat.

James simply couldn't bear it.

"If only I could get Panda back, I'd share *all* my toys with everyone!" he thought. "Oh, Panda, where are you?"

Well, Mrs Hill telephoned the laundry the next day about Panda, and what do you think they said?

"Oh, we're very sorry, Madam, but as the panda was a bit dirty, we thought you'd popped him into the laundry basket to be washed – and we're afraid he's being washed this morning."

James had to try very hard not to burst into tears when he heard this bad news. He screwed up his face and went out into the garden. He couldn't make up his mind if he wanted Panda back or not. He knew he couldn't bear a panda that had been squeezed out flat by the wringer, so that he no longer looked like his dear, fat, tubby, solid Panda. His grunt would be gone, too. It would have been squeezed out of him.

James couldn't eat any dinner or tea and Mummy became quite worried about him. "Surely you aren't still fretting about Panda?" she asked.

James didn't say anything. He wished people wouldn't talk about Panda. He knew he would dream about him all night – a horrid, long, flat Panda with no grunt left in his middle at all.

Next day a parcel arrived for James. It had the name of the laundry on it. There was a note pinned to it that Mummy opened and read.

"We are sending back the panda quickly in case your little boy wants it. He is quite clean now, and he is longing to get back home. We only gave him a light wash, and we didn't squeeze him at all."

"*Oh!*" said James, and a great load rolled away from his heart. "He hasn't been put through the wringer then, Mummy. He may look just the same."

Well, he did! He looked just a bit cleaner, and his grunt had gone a bit deeper, but he looked at James just as nicely out of his big, black eyes, and he felt just as fat and cuddly as ever.

James hugged him, and made him grunt for almost three minutes without stopping. "Dear Panda," he kept saying, "dear Panda, I thought you'd be spoiled for ever – and all because of me. Dear Panda!"

"You're lucky to have him back, after stuffing him into a laundry basket," said Mummy.

"Mummy – ask Jane to tea today, *please*," said James suddenly. "Will you?"

"But why?" asked Mummy. "You didn't seem to like her yesterday. Why do you want to see her today?"

"I want her to play with Panda," said James. "I should have thought you would have guessed that, Mummy! She's just *got* to play with Panda today."

"I quite understand," said Mummy, and she looked very pleased. "I'll ask her to come. I'll tell her you want her to."

"Tell her *Panda* wants her to as well," said James. "He's longing to play with her, he says so – just listen to him!"

"Ooooof!" said Panda at once, and Mummy hurried away to the telephone, laughing.

If you have a panda, do read him this story and see if *he* grunts, too!

The
Disappointed
Sprites

ONCE upon a time the little water sprites were very sad. They sat swinging in the rushes that grew by the side of the lake, and talked about their trouble.

"I don't think it's fair!" said Willow. "Why shouldn't we water sprites be allowed to dance in the fairy ring too? I do think that the fairies are mean!"

"Is it really true that they said we weren't to dance with them any more?" asked Trickle.

"Yes, didn't you know?" said Splashabout. "They sent us a letter this morning. Read it out to us, Willow."

Willow took a letter from her

pocket and spread it out. "This is what they say," she began. "Dear Water Sprites, please do not come and dance in our fairy ring any more. You spoil our dances. With love from the Fairies."

"Well! How very horrid of them!" cried Trickle. "Why don't they want us any more? We behave quite nicely!"

"Let's go and ask them!" said Splashabout. "And if we think their reason is fair, we won't make a fuss. But if it isn't, we'll go and complain to the Queen."

So the three little sprites set off over the grass to Pixie Town among the toadstools. Here were fairies and elves, pixies and brownies. They all stared at the three sprites as they came running up, and wondered what was the matter.

"What do you want?" they cried. "Have you lost something?"

"No," answered Willow, "but we want to know why we aren't allowed to come and dance with you any more. What have we done to upset you?"

"Nothing," said a fairy. "It isn't really your fault."

"Well, whose fault is it, then?" asked Splashabout, impatiently. "We think it really is very, very mean of you."

The pixies and fairies looked at each other. Nobody wanted to explain. At last a brownie broke the silence.

"It's like this," he said. "You're always so wet, and when we dance with you we spoil our clothes."

"And you make all the seats wet too, with your damp frocks," said an elf.

"And I've got a dreadful cold through putting on one of your wet shawls by mistake. A-tishoo! A-tishoo!" said a pixie, and blew his nose loudly.

The water sprites stared sadly

at the fairies.

"But we can't help being wet," said Trickle sorrowfully. "We live in the water, you see, so we're always wet and we never, ever get colds."

"That's because you're used to it," said a fairy. "We aren't, and we feel as if we're dancing with frogs when we dance with you. We're awfully sorry about it, but you do spoil all our dances."

The three water sprites looked at each other, and decided to be brave about it.

"We're sorry," said Willow. "We quite understand."

"But it is quite dreadfully

disappointing, because we do so like dancing," said Trickle, nearly bursting into tears.

"And there's no place on the water where we can dance," said Splashabout.

Then they said goodbye, and went sadly back to the lake. They told all the water sprites what they had heard, and everyone was very upset.

"That's the end of all our dancing," said Ripple. "It's a great pity, for we are the lightest and daintiest of all fairy folk."

"Well, we must just make the best of it," said Willow. "We'll go and watch next time the fairies have a dance, but we won't go near enough to wet them."

So next time the elves and fairies held a dance in the fairy ring, the sprites crept up to watch them. They heard the music played by the grasshoppers and bees, and longed to join in the dance, but they had made up their minds to be good – and so they were.

Carefully they hid themselves in the long grass around the fairy ring and peeped out from behind the wild flowers to watch quietly.

Now, it happened that the Fairy Queen decided to go to the dance that night. She floated down, pale and beautiful in the moonlight and took her place on the little silver throne that always stood waiting for her.

The fairies were delighted to see her, and made a great fuss of her, for she was very good to them. "Go on with your dancing," she said. "I love to watch you."

So they all danced and tripped,

and pranced and skipped, as
merry as could be, till suddenly
the Queen wondered where the
water sprites were. They had
never missed a dance before, and
she couldn't think why they
weren't there. She peeped all
round the dancers, but not one
sprite could she see.

And then she suddenly spied
them peeping and peering
behind the buttercups and
daisies outside the fairy ring! She
was astonished!

She clapped her hands and
ordered the dance to stop for a
minute. Everyone turned to hear
what Her Majesty had to say.

"Why do the water sprites peep and hide, instead of dancing?" she asked. "Have they been naughty?"

"Oh no, Your Majesty!" answered a pixie. "They're not at all naughty. We sent them a letter asking them not to come to our dances any more."

"Why did you do that?" asked the Queen in astonishment.

"Because they are always so dreadfully wet!" answered the pixie. "They ruin our clothes and make us catch terrible colds."

"But haven't they anywhere to dance now?" asked the Queen.

"No, nowhere," said the pixie.

"They can't dance on the lake, you see, and we can't have them in our dancing rings any more."

"Dear, dear!" said the Queen. "Whatever can we do! Were the water sprites nice about it, or were they angry?"

"They were ever so nice," said all the fairies at once.

"They promised not to come!" said a brownie.

"And they said they were sorry and that they quite understood!" called an elf.

The Queen was pleased. She liked to hear of people taking disappointment cheerfully. She waved her hand.

"Go on with your dancing," she said, looking thoughtful.

The bees and grasshoppers began playing again, and the fairies took their partners and went merrily on with their dance.

They didn't see the Queen slip away through the grass. She went very quietly, her crown gleaming like dewdrops in the bright moonlight.

She went to the lake. It lay very peaceful and still. All the sprites who usually played there were away watching the dance.

Big white and yellow water lillies lay on the water. The Queen called to them.

"Water lillies," she cried,
"where are your leaves?"

"Down in the water!"
answered the water lillies in
voices like a hundred singing
ripples.

"Listen!" said the Queen.
"Raise them to the top of the
lake, and let them spread
themselves smooth and flat on
the water."

The lilles all raised their leaves
and did as they were told.
Gradually the lake became
spread with big flat leaves,
shining in the moonlight.

"Thank you," said the Queen.
"You look beautiful now, water

lillies. Will you let the little water sprites dance on your leaves when the lake is calm?"

"Yes! Yes!" sang the water lillies softly. "We love the water sprites; they look after our buds for us!"

Then the Queen called the
green frogs to her, and told each
to fetch his instrument and climb
on to the water lily leaves and
play a merry tune.

"Yes, Your Majesty!" they
cried, and clambered quickly up.
Then they struck up such a loud
merry tune that all the fairies
and sprites away by the dancing
ring listened in astonishment.
Then they all ran helter-skelter
to the lake to see what the music
could be.

There they found the Queen,
sitting on a water lily, with the
frogs playing their instruments as
merrily as could be.

"Look! Look!" cried the fairies, "the water lillies have brought their leaves to the surface!"

"What fun! What fun!" cried the water sprites, jumping on to the leaves. "Oh, Your Majesty, we could dance on these leaves! May we?"

"Yes, you may," answered the Queen, smiling. "And now, whenever the fairies hold a dance in the fairy ring, you may hold a dance on the lily leaves, for the frogs will play for you until dawn!"

"Oh, thank you, thank you!" cried the sprites in great delight.

They each took a partner and were soon happily dancing on the smooth lily leaves, whilst the fairies looked on in wonder.

When dawn came, nothing was to be seen of the Queen or the fairies. The water sprites were gone, and so were the frogs and their instruments.

But calm and steady the water lily leaves floated on the water, waiting for the time when little feet should dance on them once again.

Look at them, next time you pass by a lake. The biggest leaf you see is the one that all the frogs stand on to play their instruments, and the biggest water lily is the one the Queen sits on. Don't you think it was a splendid idea of hers?

The Unkind
Little Girl

MILLIE lived in a great big house on the top of a hill. She had a nanny, a maid to look after her clothes and her very own private teacher. In her playroom were the finest and loveliest toys you could imagine – so many of them that really her playroom looked like a toy shop!

But Millie didn't love her toys. She didn't take care of her dolls or cuddle them. She didn't put them away at night. She didn't take her teddy to bed with her. She never dusted her doll's house and, as for her books, the only thing she ever did with them was to tear them.

She was an unkind little girl. If anything went wrong, she stamped and screamed, and every day she broke some of her toys. Once she threw a doll out of the playroom window and its head broke right off. Another time she trod on her bear and her pink rabbit because they wouldn't squeak loudly enough to please her.

So you can guess how afraid all her toys were of her, and how they trembled when she came into the playroom. Most toys are glad when boys and girls come to play with them, for they get bored when they are left alone –

but Millie's toys hated her and would have run away if they had dared to.

Now one day a beautiful fairy doll with wings and a crown came to the playroom. She was so lovely that all the toys fell in love with her at once.

"It's a pity you have come to this playroom," said the teddy bear to her. "Millie is such an unkind child. She is sure to break your arm or take away your golden crown."

"How dreadful!" said the fairy doll in alarm. "Oh, look – here she comes."

Millie came in. She was in a

very bad temper that day because her teacher had made her learn the six times table and had kept her in until it was all learnt. Millie was a lazy girl and she didn't like learning anything. So she wore a frown on her face and she stamped straight into the playroom as if she were a cart-horse.

"Quietly, quietly, Millie," said the nanny, who was sewing in a corner. "Be careful with your toys, now – you left them all lying about the floor this morning and you'll tread on them if you don't look where you are going!"

"I don't care if I *do* tread on them!" said Millie crossly, and she stamped on a brick and broke it. Then she trod on a little clockwork mouse and broke that. She threw open her toy cupboard door and swept everything out on to the floor in a temper.

Crash! Smash! Crash! Goodness, what a mess! There was a little doll with a broken nose – a clockwork rabbit whose leg was knocked off in his fall – two books whose pages were bent – another doll whose toes were chipped as she fell feet first – and the fairy doll with her crown knocked off and a wing torn. Oh dear, what a lot of damage was done, to be sure, when the bad tempered little girl swept all her toys out of the cupboard in a hurry.

"Millie! Millie! What *are* you doing!" cried her nanny in alarm. "Just look at your toys! You have broken half of them. It's unkind and horrid of you."

"I don't care," said Millie crossly. "Toys are meant to be broken."

"Oh, no they are not," said Nanny, picking up the poor toys and putting them back into the cupboard. "They are meant to be played with and loved."

That night, when Millie had gone to bed, the fairy doll picked up her crown and put it back on her head. She looked very angry. She smoothed out her torn wing and then looked round at the other toys.

"Toys!" she said in a little tinkling voice, "Toys! I will not stay here with this horrid child. I am going away. Who will come with me?"

"I will!" cried everyone at once and all the toys stood up together. Even the bricks and books cried out too, and the fairy doll was pleased.

"No child as unkind as Millie

ought to have toys." said the fairy doll. "Now listen – I have an idea. I know that there is to be a party for poor children in the church hall not far from here. There will be a big tub full of toys for the children. It's a lucky dip. The tub is filled with sawdust and the children put their hands in, take out a parcel, undo it and find a toy inside which they keep. Shall we all go to the hall and hide ourselves in that tub?"

"Yes, yes!" cried the toys. "But how can we all get there? The bricks and books can't walk."

"I have just a little magic in my

wand," said the fairy doll. "It's only a very little, but I think it will be enough to help us. I will wave it and wish for little legs to grow on every toy that cannot walk. Then you will all please follow me and we'll go away from here."

She waved her wand. Goodness, what a strange thing happened! Every brick, every book, every ball, even the wooden spade and tin pail, grew little legs! It was a funny sight to see them all running about here and there.

"Get into line, now," ordered the fairy doll. "I know the way, and you must all follow me. It's a fine, moonlit night and we shall be able to see our way very clearly."

So off they all started. They first of all climbed out of the playroom window and then walked down the garden path to the front gate. The fairy doll led the way with the other dolls close behind. Then came the teddy bears, the rabbits and the big sailor doll. After that came the clockwork toys, which had all been carefully wound up. Then came the bricks, the balls, the spade and pail, the books and one or two other toys.

Nobody saw the toys going down the road except the policeman who stood at the corner. He was so astonished that he couldn't move a step, but just stood there with his mouth wide open in surprise. The toys slipped in at the big iron gate that led to the church hall, and by the time the policeman ran after them they had disappeared. So he thought he must have dreamed them!

The toys marched into the hall and went to the lucky dip tub. Near it was a big pile of brown paper and string. The teddy bear said he would wrap up the toys in

parcels and do himself last of all.
So he set to work and soon every
one of the toys was made into a
paper parcel and had been
tucked deep down into the tub.
Last of all the teddy bear
wrapped himself up, but he
couldn't tie the string. So he
squeezed down into the sawdust
with just a bit of brown paper
rolled round him.

Well, next day, when the poor
children came along to the party,
they were delighted to see there
was a lucky dip. The lady who
was looking after it wished that
she had had more toys to put in
the tub, for there were more

children than she had expected. So you can guess how surprised she was to find so many toys there when the children came along to dip into it.

"Dear me!" she said, when the teddy bear was drawn up, and a parcel of bricks, books and other toys. "Dear me! Someone must have put some more toys in after I had gone home last night! There are such a lot of really *nice* toys! How pleased the children will be!"

So they were! They went home with their toys, hugging and cuddling them and shouting to their mothers that they were the best and nicest toys they had ever had.

"We will treat them well and take care of them!" said all the children. How glad the toys were to hear that!

And what about Millie when she came to her playroom the next morning to play with her toys? Ah, you should have seen her face when she opened her toy cupboard door and found it quite empty! Not a brick was there, not a doll, not a single book. Everything was gone, and the cupboard was bare.

Then Millie began to cry, and her nanny came running to see

what the matter was. When she saw the empty cupboard she shook her head.

"I expect your toys have gone away to someone who will care for them and love them," she said. "Well, I don't blame them. I've a good mind to go away and leave you, too. I would like a kind, good-tempered little girl to look after instead of you, Millie."

"No, don't go, don't go!" begged Millie, holding on to her nanny's hand. "I will be kind now, really I will. I won't ever hurt a toy again."

Tomorrow her mother is going to buy her some more toys for

her empty cupboard. I wonder if Millie will keep her promise? I expect she will, because she won't want her toys to run away again. I think she has learned her lesson, don't you?

The Little Box
of Beads

ALL the toys in the nursery belonged to Polly and Dennis. The dolls and the doll's house belonged to Polly, and the bricks, the motor cars and the fire engine belonged to Dennis. All the rest of the toys they shared between them – except the box of beads.

Grandma had given the children the beads. But Dennis didn't want them. He thought it was silly for a boy to thread beads, so he told Polly she could have them.

But, you know, they were such teeny-tiny beads that Polly soon got tired of threading them. It

took ages to make even a small
bracelet because the beads were
so very small, and besides, the
needle she used to thread them
with kept pricking her finger. So
she gave it up.

Mummy put the beads at the
back of the toy cupboard. "They
may come in useful some day,"
she said. So they lay there and it
wasn't long before the two
children forgot all about them.

But the toys knew all about
those beads! The monkey had
lifted the lid off the box one
night to peep in at the beads, and
he called out to the other toys to
come and see them.

"They are so pretty!" he said. "Look! Red and blue and white and pink and yellow and purple! Aren't they small! Oh, I do wish we could thread them, don't you, toys? They would make such pretty necklaces for the dolls."

"No, we mustn't use them," said Esmeralda, the walking doll. "They belong to Polly. We might upset the box and that would be a pity."

The monkey went on looking at them. Then he dabbled his hand in the beads and let them run through his fingers. He did so want to thread some! But he knew that he must obey

Esmeralda, because she was the biggest toy in the nursery, so he shut the lid. But as he did so his sleeve caught the edge of the box – and it slipped off the shelf!

Over it went on to the floor and all the beads spilt out. Then, what a hunt the toys had for them! They spent all night long looking for them in every corner, and at last the had found them all except a little red bead that had rolled into a mouse hole and couldn't be reached by anyone.

"Now we'd better put the box back again and not touch it any more," said Esmeralda. "No, you mustn't put it back, Monkey –

you'd be sure to upset it again, you're so clumsy."

So it was put back on the shelf again and there it lay getting dustier and dustier each day.

Now one night, when the toys were playing hide-and-seek in the playroom, they heard the sound of somebody crying. They stopped to listen.

"It's somebody outside," said the teddy bear. "Let's peep out of the window and see who it is."

They ran to the window and peeped out. There was bright moonlight outside and they could see quite clearly. On the grass sat two small creatures,

both with long silvery wings.
They were sobbing bitterly.

"Hey!" called the bear,
anxiously. "What's the matter?
Have you hurt yourselves?"

The two little creatures looked
up. They were pixies, and had
small pointed faces with little
sticking-out ears. They gave a
shriek of fright when they saw
the bear.

"It's all right, I'm only a toy
bear," said the teddy, kindly.
"Come into the nursery and tell
us what's the matter."

The pixies flew up to the
window-sill and slipped into the
playroom. They were dressed in

frocks of grey spider's web, fine but very plain.

"Good evening, toys," they said politely. "We're sorry if we disturbed you."

"Not at all," said Esmeralda. "What were you crying for? Had somebody been nasty to you?"

"Oh no," said one pixie. "We were crying because our lovely necklaces are gone. You should have seen them! They were beautiful!"

"We made them ourselves," said the second pixie. "We got some tiny millet seeds and painted them all colours. Then we threaded them on spider thread. They looked lovely with our plain grey frocks."

"Well, what happened to them?" asked the teddy bear.

"Oh, a dreadful thing happened," said the first pixie. "We went to sleep with our necklaces round our necks, under one of those big toadstools by the oak tree in the garden – and whilst we were asleep two little mice came and ate our necklaces away! They love millet seed, you know – so when we woke up our necklaces were gone!"

"And we're going to a dance under the beech tree in the

garden tonight and to another one on Saturday night too!" said the other pixie, beginning to cry again. "But how can we go in these old grey frocks, without any beads? We haven't got any other frocks. The beads made us look cheerful and pretty."

"Yes, you certainly want something to cheer up those plain grey frocks," said Esmeralda. "What about a sash? Perhaps I could lend you mine."

"Or you can have the red ribbon off my neck," said the bear, beginning to untie it.

"Or my best yellow bow!" said the plush duck.

"No!" cried the monkey suddenly. "No! I know what would be best of all! New necklaces made of those small coloured beads in the bead box on the cupboard shelf! That would be lovely."

"Oh, yes! Oh, yes!" shouted all the toys in delight. "Just the thing! Just the VERY thing!"

"But we can't use them without asking Polly, can we?" said Esmeralda. "They're her beads and they belong to her."

"Well, let's go and ask her about them, then!" cried the monkey. "I'll go!"

And off he went to the

children's bedroom before anyone could stop him! Polly was sleeping there in one corner, and Dennis was sleeping in the other. They were both fast asleep.

The monkey stole up to Polly's bed and gave the bedclothes a tug. Polly didn't wake. He made a little scraping noise on her pillow. Still she didn't wake. Then he lightly touched her arm and whispered: "Polly! Polly!"

Polly woke up with a jump. She sat up in bed and there, by the light of the moon, she saw the monkey's anxious little face looking up at her.

"Sh!" he said. "Don't wake

anyone else. I've come to ask you something. May we use those beads out of the little bead box to make two necklaces for some pixies who have lost theirs? Do say yes!"

At first Polly was too surprised to say anything. Then she nodded her head and spoke softly.

"Yes!" she whispered. "Use as many as you like and make two beautiful necklaces. Give my love to the pixies."

The monkey was so pleased. He ran off quietly and soon told the toys and the pixies what Polly had said. They found the

bead box in delight and took off
the lid. Then the monkey did
what he always longed and
longed to do – he threaded those
tiny coloured beads into
beautiful necklaces!

You should have seen him! How carefully he did it! One after another the little coloured beads slipped over the needle and down the silk thread – and at last the necklaces were finished. The pixies tried them on with little cries of delight. The colourful beads shone brightly against their dull grey frocks and both pixies looked lovely!

"Oh, thank you, thank you!" they cried. "It is so kind of you! Now we can go to the dance and look our very best. Perhaps the King himself will dance with us when he sees our lovely bead necklaces! Please thank Polly very much indeed – and give her this from us!"

They put a card into the monkey's hand, and then flew happily off on their silvery wings.

The monkey put the card into the bead box for safety and then he and the toys played leap-frog until the dawn came creeping in at the window.

When Polly woke up next day she remembered how she had woken up in the night and seen the monkey. She told Dennis all about it – but of course he didn't believe her.

"You're making it up!" he said. "Or else you dreamt it. Don't be silly, Polly – you know it can't possibly be true."

"Well, it is so!" said Polly quite crossly. "I'm just going to look into the bead box and see if any beads are gone. If they are, then I shall know it wasn't a dream."

She got the bead box and opened it – and she saw that half the beads were gone! She saw something else too – a little card in the box with something written on it. She took it out.

The she gave a cry of surprise – for what do you suppose was written on the card? This:

"The pixies will be glad to see Polly and friend at the dance under the beech tree in the back garden on Saturday at twelve o'clock midnight."

"Look, look, Dennis!" she cried, and she showed him the card. "Oh, how lovely! The two pixies that the monkey told me about must have left the card in the box. Oh, do let's go! You can go too, because it says: 'Polly and friend'."

Well, of course, Dennis had to believe it after that! Besides, he badly wanted to go with Polly, and he didn't want her to take anybody else instead of him. So they're both going on Saturday night. They will know the pixies when they see them because they will look out for the two necklaces made of the tiny beads that Grandma gave them. I do wish I were Polly, don't you?

When the Sun Rises

IT was night-time. Everywhere was dark. The little birds were all asleep in the trees and hedges, and the rabbits were down in their holes. Only the red fox was out, hunting, and the big owl hooted as it looked for mice in the fields.

"The night is very long," said a little sparrow to his brother.

"It will soon be over now," said his brother.

"It is very cold," said a thrush, waking up and stretching his brown wings.

"When the sun rises it will be warm," said the blackbird.

A small rabbit put his head out

of his burrow.

"I can see a grey light in the sky!" he called to his mother.

"Come here," said his mother. "The red fox is about. Wait till the sun rises and then you can go out safely, for the fox will go to his hole then."

The grey light in the sky grew brighter. Then slowly, slowly it turned to pale gold – then to bright gold – the sun was coming!

"Chirrup-chirrup-chirrup!" twittered the sparrows, waking up one after another. "The sun is rising!"

The blackbird opened his

orange beak and sang a song to welcome the sun. "The night was cold, so cold!" he sang. "But now the sky is gold!"

"Come and see, come and see, come and see!" sang the freckled thrush.

"Look, look!" cried the little rabbit, running out of his hole on the grass. "Here comes the big, round, golden sun!"

All the birds looked. Many rabbits came from their holes and watched. Some butterflies sleeping on the flowers awoke, stretched their pretty wings and fluttered up into the air to see the golden sun come slipping up into the sky. What a big, round ball it looked! How bright it was! How warm!

"The sky is red and gold!" called the starling from the tree-top. "The little clouds are red and gold too. I wish I had feathers of red and gold! How beautiful I should be!"

The rabbits scampered out into the early sunshine. They nibbled the grass. They were delighted to welcome the sun.

A lark awoke in the field. He felt the warmth of the rising sun on his brown feathers. He lifted up the crest on his head in delight. He had his nest in the field and his wife and babies were there. He was happy.

"Here is the beautiful sun again!" he sang to his wife. "I must fly up, up, up into the sky to get as near him as I can, and tell him all about our dear little family."

So up he flew into the sky, up and up until the rabbits could only see a little black speck. But they could hear his beautiful song. It came pouring down from the sky as the lark flew higher and higher.

"I love the sun, the sun, the sun," he sang. "It warms my little ones, it makes the world so bright and lovely, I love the shining sun!"

"Pink, pink!" said the pretty little chaffinch, waking up in the hedge. "The clouds are pink, pink! The sun has risen again. It is day-time!"

The two robins flew to the

hedgetop and sang their creamy song of joy. "Here is another lovely day. The sun went away last night and left the world dark and cold. Now he is back again and everything is beautiful! We love the sun!"

The Big Fur Monkey

THERE was once a very handsome monkey. He was made of pink fur and he had fine glass eyes, a long pink tail, and a most beautiful spotted bow. The inside of his ears was green, and he could squeak very loudly if you pressed him in the middle.

He lived on the bottom shelf in the toy shop, and he was very proud of himself indeed, for he was the biggest and best monkey in the shop. He cost a lot of money – so much that nobody bought him for a long time.

All the toys knew him well and were a little afraid of him because he was so grand. They didn't like him very much because he was boastful.

"When *I'm* sold I shall go to live in a palace, I expect," he often used to say. "I shall belong to a rich little girl or boy and I shall be treated with great care and given a doll's bed to lie on and an armchair of my own. Ah, you poor toys, you don't no how grand I shall be!"

"And we don't care either," said the brown teddy bear, who was very tired of hearing all the monkey's boasting.

The monkey frowned and said no more. He thought the other toys were not worth talking to.

One day a rich little girl came into the shop with her nanny. All the toys sat straight up and looked at her – but she didn't look so very nice. She had a sulky face and was always rude to her nanny.

"Now which toy would you like?" said her nanny kindly. "It's your birthday, so you can choose whichever you like."

"I want something that costs a lot of money," said the little girl.

"Well, here is a doll. She costs nineteen pounds," said the shop woman, taking down a pretty golden-haired doll.

"I've got lots of dolls, thank

you," said the little girl, looking round the shop. "What about that pink monkey? I don't have a monkey at home. How much does he cost?"

"He costs twenty five pounds," said the woman. "He is a very beautiful monkey."

"I want him, Nanny," said the little girl. "He looks very pretty. He can sleep in my doll's cot at night, and I've a nice little deck-chair that will just fit him."

Well, you should have seen how the pink monkey swelled with pride when he heard that! Hadn't he always said he would be bought by a rich little girl and

live in a grand house and be
treated well? Now all the toys
could see that he was right!

The shop woman wrapped him
up and the little girl took him
home. She sat him in her small
deck-chair and he felt very
grand. He looked round at the
other toys in the playroom. They
seemed very old and battered.

"I don't think much of *you*!"
said the monkey in disgust.
"What dreadful broken things
you look!"

"Well, you won't look much
better soon," said a doll with a
broken nose. "You've no idea
what a horrid little girl Mary is!

She throws us about, stamps on us and breaks us whenever she is in a bad temper – which is nearly every day!"

"Good gracious!" said the monkey in alarm. "Well, *I* won't stand such behaviour!"

The very next day, when Mary came into the playroom, she was in a bad temper and began to throw her toys about. She took the monkey from his chair and trod on him! He squeaked loudly, of course, and the little girl heard him and jumped up and down harder and harder, making him squeak more and more loudly.

At last his squeak broke and he could make no more noise. Then Mary flung him out of the window and he fell into the street below, right in the gutter.

It was muddy. The poor monkey lay half in water, and felt himself getting wet.

He was very unhappy. To think that he, the most beautiful monkey that lived in the toy shop, should have been stamped on, and then flung into the gutter! He could have cried out loud with shame.

Presently an old woman came along. She saw the monkey lying there in the wet gutter, and she picked him up.

"Some child's dropped you, I suppose," she said. "Well, you aren't much to look at, all dirty and wet. I'll take you home and dry you, and if you're worth it, which seems unlikely, I'll give you away to someone."

She stuffed him into her basket with potatoes and cabbages. The potatoes made him dirtier than ever, and a large green caterpillar crawled out of a cabbage onto his nose. It was dreadful. At last the old woman arrived home. She emptied her bag out on to the table.

"Good gracious!" she said,

when she saw how dirty the toy monkey was. "You're not fit to be given away at all. I'd better put you into the dustbin straightaway."

The monkey could hardly believe his ears. Put into the dustbin! A monkey like him, who had cost twenty-five pounds and been the finest toy in the shop! He tried to squeak angrily, but his squeak was broken.

After a while the old woman picked him up and looked at him. "I'll just give you a wash," she said. "If I can get you a bit cleaner, maybe you won't look quite so bad."

To the monkey's horror, she held him under a hot-water tap and nearly scalded him, the water was so hot. Then she shook him well, squeezed him, and took him out into the garden. She took two pegs and pegged the poor wet monkey up on to the clothes-line by his ears! What do you think of that?

He was so ashamed, so very unhappy. To think that he, such a grand monkey, should have come to this!

The sun came out and warmed him. The wind blew and dried him. His fur had gone hard and tangled, his ears were out of shape, his tail was loose. He really was a funny sight.

The old woman came out and unpegged him. She brushed him hard with a clothes-brush and then looked at him. "Well," she said, "you're not much to look at, but I dare say Mrs Brown's children will be pleased to have you. There are six of them and they only have two toys between them! I'll take you along to them this very minute!"

Off she went with the monkey. He trembled when he thought of six children with so few toys. What would happen to him now? He would be stamped on, thrown about, struck, smacked.....oh, dear, what a dreadful fate!

The six children were delighted to see the monkey. The eldest child of the six was nine, the youngest was one.

"Oh, isn't he just beautiful!" cried Peter.

"Isn't he nice and cuddly!" shouted Mollie.

"I do love him! He's wonderful!" said little Jean.

"I want him for my own!" said Eileen. Nobody was rough with him. Everybody stroked him and made a fuss of him.

"You shall each have him for a day and a night in turn," said

Mrs Brown, their mother. "He is a nice monkey and you must treat him well."

So each child had the monkey for a day and a night. First Peter played with him, took him out and showed him proudly to all the other children in the street – and at night he took the monkey to bed and cuddled him lovingly. Then Mollie had her turn and then all the others.

The monkey was very happy. He had lost his grand ideas, and had forgotten to be boastful and vain. The children loved him and he loved them. He didn't mind living with them at all, they were so kind to him. Nobody ever stamped on him. Nobody threw him out of the window as Mary had done.

One day he lost a glass eye and Mrs Brown sewed a black boot button in its place. He looked a bit strange, but the children loved him just the same. Another time he lost half his tail and an ear – but still the children thought he was the most beautiful monkey in the whole world. He slept in bed each night with one of them and was always being cuddled.

It happened one morning that the children took him into the

park. There was another child there, with his mother, and this child had a teddy bear which was sitting on the seat whilst the little boy played. The Brown children put their monkey on the seat by the bear. They looked at one another.

"Why, aren't you the brown teddy bear that lived in the shop with me?" cried the monkey.

"Yes," said the bear, looking in astonishment at the poor battered monkey. "But it can't really be you, Pink Monkey? You look dreadful! I thought at least you had gone to live in a palace with a rich little girl – but here you are with a pack of dirty children, even dirtier than they are! You've a boot-button eye and only one ear! I am ashamed to be seen talking to you! Aren't you ashamed to be owned by such children?"

The monkey laughed.

"Oh, I was foolish in my young days!" he said. "I had a bed of my own, and a chair, and a rich little girl to play with – but I had no love, no kindness. These children may be poor and dirty, but they know how to be kind, they know how to love. I love them too. I don't want to be grand any more, I don't want to

live with a rich little girl! The
only things that matter, Brown
Bear, whether you are a child or
a toy, are love and kindness, and
just you remember that! I love
others and make them happy,
and they love me and make *me*
happy. What more can anyone
want than that?"

"You are wrong and foolish!"
said the bear, turning away his
head. "I really don't think I wish
to talk to a dreadful-looking
creature like you."

But all the same the pink
monkey was right, wasn't he?
Those children have still got him,
and though he has lost *all* his tail

now, and isn't in the least bit pink any longer, he doesn't care. He is still cuddled and loved, so he is perfectly happy, poor old battered fur monkey!

I Shall Sit Here

THERE was once a daisy seed that flew on the wind and came to rest in a garden. It fell on a lawn where the children played, and settled down there.

It put out a tiny root and a tiny shoot, and began to grow. The shoot grew two little leaves that reached up into the sunshine.

Then the grass round about spoke crossly: "Get away from here, daisy plant! A lawn is a lawn, and should only be grass. Daisies and clover and thistles are not welcome here. Get away and grow somewhere else."

"I can't," said the daisy. "Don't be unkind. I haven't runners like the strawberry plants have, that can run about all over the place, growing new little strawberry plants where they like. I want to be here. It's a children's lawn, and children like daisies better than grass."

"Well, we shall grow thickly round you and smother you with hundreds of our little green blades," said the grass. "We shall stop you getting the light and the sun, and you will die!"

So the grass grew closely all round the tiny daisy plant, and it had hardly any room to grow at all. It was very upset, and called to a tiny ladybird running by.

"What can I do to grow safely in this lawn? The grass is trying to choke me!"

"I'll go and ask the thistles I know," said the ladybird, spreading her wings out. "There are some growing on the tennis lawn, though they know they are not allowed there. I'll see how they manage it."

In a few minutes the ladybird was back. "The thistle says it's quite easy. You are to sit down hard on the lawn, spread out your leaves firmly in a rosette, and tell the grass you are going to stay there," she said.

"Oh, thank you," said the

daisy. "I'll do what you say."

Its leaves were now well grown. It had been holding them up in the air, out of the way of the grass, but now it put them down firmly on the grass itself. It arranged them cleverly in a rosette all round itself, so that the grass blades beneath could not get any air or light, and had to move themselves away from the daisy.

"I shall sit here," said the little plant to the grass around. "I shall spread out my leafy skirts and sit down here. This is my own little place. Keep away, grass, or I shall sit on you!"

The grass grumbled, but it couldn't do anything about it! It had to keep away from the firm rosette of daisy leaves, or be smothered! The daisy sent up tight little round buds, which opened in the sun. They spread out pink tipped petals, with a round golden eye at the centre.

"That is how I get my name – day's eye – daisy!" said the daisy.

The children found the little daisy plant as they sat on the lawn, playing. "Oh, look!" said Peter. "Daisies! Let's pick some, and put them in a tiny vase for Mummy."

"Yes, let's," said Jane. "I love

daisies. They seem to look at us with their golden eyes. I'm glad there are some on our lawn. I'm surprised the grass lets them grow here!"

"Aha!" thought the daisy. "I know the trick of growing in grass now. All I need to do is to say 'I shall sit here,' and arrange my leaves in a rosette – then I can grow anywhere!"

It's quite true – that's what a daisy plant always does. You look and see the next time you are out in your garden!

Hurry up,
George!

THAT boy's so slow I believe he'd let a snail race him!" said George's mother. "George! How long am I going to wait for you to bring me in the washing?"

George brought in the washing, dropping half of it on the way. "Oh, do hurry up, George," said his mother. "I thought you wanted to paint the fence green for me this morning! Well, there won't be any time soon."

"Oh, my," said George. "Yes, I did want to do some painting, Ma. I like painting. The brush goes slap-slap-slap, and the paint looks so nice."

"Well, I told you that you

would only have till lunch-time
to paint the fence," said his
mother. "We have to catch the
bus to go to market this
afternoon, and then we shan't be
home till six. So all of your
painting will have to be done
pretty quickly!"

"Yes. I can paint quickly," said
George, making up his mind he
would get the fence done before
his lunch.

He went out with the pot of
green paint and a big brush. He
remembered to put on his
overalls. He looked at the fence.
It wasn't a very big one, and half
of it was already painted. George

dipped his brush into the pot.

Slap-slap-slap! The brush slapped on the bright paint, and the fence began to look nice. But, of course, George soon began to feel tired, and he painted more and more slowly. Slapitty-slap! The brush didn't slap on the paint so fast now, and when George's mother looked out of the window, she saw George about to sit down and have a rest.

"Do hurry up, George!" she called. "You will never have time to finish before lunch."

"Well, I'll have to finish tomorrow, then," said George.

"That's what you always say to everything!" called his mother. "Tomorrow, tomorrow, tomorrow – never today. Get *on*, George!"

Little Stephen came by, and he stood and watched George beginning to paint again. He called to George's mother.

"Good morning! Your cooking smells nice."

"I suppose, as usual, you've had no breakfast, and you won't have lunch either!" said George's mother, who was sorry for hungry little Stephen. "George – you've stopped painting again. You'll never finish it before it's time for us to have our lunch!"

"Shall I help him?" asked Stephen.

"No. There's only one brush," said George's mother. "Look, Stephen – if you can somehow make George finish the fence in time, you can stay and have lunch with us!"

"Ooooh!" said Stephen, and his eyes gleamed. He looked at George. How in the world could he make George hurry? If he told him he was being slow, George would only say there was plenty of time tomorrow.

Then he grinned to himself. He looked into the paint pot. He stirred the paint round with a stick. He lifted up the pot and put it down again.

"What are you doing?" asked George, surprised.

"George – you haven't much paint left," said Stephen, solemnly. "Do you know what's going to happen if you don't hurry? Your paint pot will be empty before you've finished your fence."

"Good gracious," said George, alarmed. "Then I'd better paint very, very quickly, hadn't I, in case the paint runs out before I've finished?"

"Yes," said Stephen, with a grin. "You paint at top speed,

George, and maybe your paint will last out. Go on, now."

And you should just have seen George painting at top speed then! He had finished the fence five minutes before lunch-time, and there was still a spot of paint in the pot. George was pleased.

"Ma! I've been so quick that I've finished before my paint ran out!" he called – and how his mother smiled.

"Come along in to lunch, both of you," she called. "There's an extra big helping for you, George, because you've been so quick – and a great big one for you, Stephen, because you've been so very smart!"

"Smart? How has he been smart?" said George. "*I* don't know!"

But you know, don't you? *You* wouldn't have been taken in by crafty little Stephen, would you?

The Foolish Frog

THERE was once a frog who was really very foolish. He thought he knew everything. When he was a tadpole he swam round telling everyone what nasty, leggy things frogs were – but even when he found that he was growing into a frog himself that didn't make him ashamed of his foolishness! No, he just went on being as boastful and as stupid as ever.

In the autumn, when the nights were frosty, the frogs began to think of going to sleep at the bottom of the pond, head downwards in the oozy mud. The toads hopped slowly out of the water and went to some damp stones they knew. They crept underneath, shut their bright, coppery eyes and went to sleep there. They would not wake up until the warm springtime.

But the foolish frog thought it was a waste of time to sleep through so many months. He didn't want to snooze under a stone. He didn't want to sleep in the mud at the bottom of the pond. No – he wanted to be up and about like the rabbits and the mice!

"It is a stupid idea to sleep so much of your lives away!" he said to the other frogs, when they told him it was time to prepare for the winter sleep. "Why should you be afraid of the winter? What does it matter if it is cold? I shan't mind!"

"You think you are so clever!" said the other frogs scornfully. "Very well – keep awake all the winter through if it pleases you! We shan't mind!"

So they left the foolish frog, swam down to the bed of the pond, tucked themselves into the mud and were soon sound asleep. They forgot the cold, they forgot the lack of flies and grubs – they slept peacefully and happily.

But the foolish frog still swam about in the pond. He wondered where the flies had gone that used to skim on the surface, and which tasted so good. He climbed out of the water and went to look for some in the ditch. But there were no flies, no caterpillars, no slugs to be found. The little frog felt very hungry.

He went back to the water and swam round sadly. Perhaps it would be a good idea after all to go to sleep. It wasn't much good being awake and hungry!

"Well, I'll go and have a nap in the mud," said the foolish frog at last. "But I shall NOT sleep all the winter through, as the others do. No – at the first possible moment, when the sun is warm, I shall wake up and begin to enjoy myself again!"

He was soon asleep. He slept all through the month of December, and almost all through January. Then there came a warm spell. The sun shone down on the pond and frogs felt the warmth and stirred in their sleep. The foolish frog woke right up. Ah! How warm the water felt! Surely the winter was over!

He swam up to the surface. It was lovely in the sunshine. He

swam down to the mud and
woke up all the other frogs.

"Come!" he said. "The winter
is over! The sun is shining. Wake
up, and come and play."

But the oldest frog, after he
had taken one look out of the
water, swam back to the mud.

"Take no notice of the foolish
one," he said. "Winter is not
over. This is just a warm spell. It
will be colder than ever soon.
Bury your heads in the mud
again, brothers and sisters, and
go to sleep."

The frogs obeyed him – all but
the foolish frog, who was very
angry. He swam up to the surface

by himself and enjoyed the warm sunshine – but, when night came, and the sun went, something strange happened to the pond. The water became hard instead of soft, and icy cold. The pond was freezing! The water was turning into ice! The frog did not know what was happening and he was frightened. He swam round, but every minute it became more difficult.

The moon came out and shone on the freezing pond. It shone on the poor, foolish frog, now held tightly in the thickening ice. The frog opened his mouth and croaked mournfully.

A wandering hedgehog heard him and was surprised. A frog croaking at this time of year! How could that be? He peered about and saw the frog in the ice. He pattered across the hard pond and breathed down on the trapped frog.

"Friend, you are in a bad way," said the hedgehog. "You will be dead by morning unless I can help you. If I lie down by you I may melt the ice a little. Then you must struggle hard and kick out with your legs, and maybe you will get free of the ice."

The heat of the hedgehog's body thawed the ice a little and

the frog found that he was able
to move round. He kicked out
strongly with his legs and
managed to get free. In a trice he
was hopping on the icy pond, and
the hedgehog hurried away to
the bank beside him.

"There is an old stone here in
the ditch," said the kindly
hedgehog. "Get under that and
sleep for the rest of the winter,
frog. You should not be awake
now."

"Thank you," said the frog,
humbly, for once really ashamed
of himself, and very much
frightened at his narrow escape.

He crept under the stone, shut

his eyes and fell soundly asleep.

He was awakened by the croaking of the frogs in the pond. It was springtime now, and they had all awakened in excitement, glad to think the warm days had come again. They wondered where the foolish frog had gone.

"I expect he got frozen into the ice and is dead," said the oldest frog, scornfully. "He was foolish enough for anything!"

That made the foolish frog very angry. He hopped out from his stone and stared rudely at the old frog.

"No, I was not frozen into the ice," he croaked, untruthfully. "I had a very much finer winter than you did!"

"Oh, there is the foolish frog after all!" croaked all the other frogs in surprise. "Come into the pond and play, brother. Choose a nice little wife for yourself so that she may lay you eggs to grow into tadpoles!"

"I shall find a little pond where no other frogs are!" said the foolish frog. "My wife shall lay her eggs there, and we shall know that all the tadpoles in our little pond are ours! We shall teach them not to speak to or play with your tadpoles!"

With that he hopped off. Soon

he met a pretty little green frog and asked her to be his wife. Then they went to find a nice little pond where she could lay her eggs.

The foolish frog found a large puddle left by the rain. "This will do nicely," he said to his green wife. "Come along!"

The little green frog laid many eggs in the puddle. The two frogs lived there contentedly, though all the toads and frogs that passed laughed at them scornfully.

The sun shone out warmly. The puddle grew smaller as the sun dried it. It grew smaller still. The little green frog became afraid and hopped off to the big pond. But the foolish frog stayed with the jelly-like eggs, hoping that they would soon hatch.

The puddle grew very small indeed – and then, alas, it dried up altogether! The mass of frog-spawn dried up too, and the foolish frog was left in a hole by the side of the lane that led to the pond.

But still he would not move. He waited for the puddle to fill again. Soon, down the lane, there came the sound of clip-clopping hooves. The old farm horse was coming. She came nearer to the hole – nearer and nearer. One of her great hooves trod on the mass of dried frog-spawn and another almost squashed the frightened frog to bits. He leapt out of the way and only his left hind foot was hurt.

Full of fear he hopped away to the pond and leapt into the cool water. His foot hurt him and he had lost his eggs – they would never hatch now. He was ashamed and miserable.

"Here is the foolish frog back again!" croaked all the others. "Well, brother, did your eggs hatch into tadpoles in that puddle? Have you told them not to speak to our young ones!"

The foolish frog said nothing. He sank down to the mud and lay there, his foot aching.

"I am indeed foolish," he thought to himself. "I thought I knew everything, but I know nothing. I will be humble in future and listen to what the others say."

Now he is no longer proud and foolish. He does what he is told. He listens to the older frogs. He is becoming wise and humble. Soon he will no longer be known as the foolish frog.

But you will always be able to tell him by his left hind foot. It

got better but it grew crooked; so
if you see a frog with a foot like
that you will know that he once
was the little foolish frog!

A Pennyworth
of Kindness

ONCE George was on a bus going home, when a little girl got on and sat beside him. She felt in her pocket for her money, and then she looked very scared.

She sat quite still, and George wondered what was the matter. He soon knew, when the conductor came up. George gave him his money, and got his ticket – but the little girl began to cry.

"I must get out at the next stop," she told the conductor. "I must walk home. I haven't got my money in my pocket. I must have lost it."

"Now look here," said the

conductor, who was a cross-looking fellow, "you're the third child who's told me that story today, and..."

"But I really have lost it," said the little girl. "I've got a hole in my pocket."

"Look – I can pay your fare," said George, and he put some money into the little girl's hand. "My uncle gave me this yesterday, and you can have it."

"Oh, thank you!" said the little girl, and she gave it to the conductor, and he handed her a ticket. "You are kind. What's your name? I'll give it back to you when Mummy gives me my pocket-money."

"My name's George," the little
boy said. "But I don't want the
money back. You can have it.
I've got some more at home."

"All the same, I shall pay you
back for your pennyworth of
kindness," said the little girl.
That made George laugh. A
pennyworth of kindness really
sounded funny.

The little girl ran home to her
mother, when she got out at her
stop. She told her all about
George and his kindness.

"Well, that's really nice of the
boy," said her mother. "I wonder
who he is, Mollie?"

But she couldn't find out, and Mollie never saw him on the bus again. She was worried about the money that she hadn't paid back.

"What shall I do, Mummy?" she said. "I must do something – and I've just had a birthday, so I've got lots of money."

"Well, dear, if you can't pay the bit of kindness back to George, you can always pay it to someone else who needs it," said her mother. "Look out for someone."

So Mollie looked out, and she soon found somebody. It was old Mrs Forrester. Mollie saw her coming along the road, carrying a basket. Just as she came up to Mollie, the old lady slipped and fell. Her basket fell, too, and there was a little crashing sound.

"Oh dear, oh dear!" said Mrs Forrester, picking herself up. "There go my eggs! It's all right, little girl, I haven't hurt myself – but I've cracked my precious eggs – and I've no money to go and buy more!"

"I've got some money! I'll buy you some more, Mrs Forrester!" cried Mollie, seeing that here was a chance for her to pay the bit of kindness she owed. She raced off to the farm, explained what had happened, and bought four more eggs for fifty pence. She went to Mrs Forrester's house and gave them to her.

"No, no," said the old lady. "I can't take them, Mollie dear. You're too kind."

"I'm not," said Mollie. "I'm only paying back a pennyworth of kindness I got from a boy called George, but as I've got a lot of money just now, I've made it a fifty pence!"

"Fifty penceworth of kindness!" said Mrs Forrester, and she laughed. "What a funny idea – and what a good one! I owe you fifty penceworth of kindness, Mollie."

"You don't need to pay it back to me, you can easily pay it to somebody else, just as I've done," said Mollie.

Mrs Forrester quite meant to pay it back to Mollie, but she fell ill after that, and had no money to pay back anything to anyone. Her brother came to see her, and as he was both kind and well-off, he paid all her bills and took her off to his home.

"Do you owe any more money to anyone?" he asked his sister, as he put her into his car to take her away with him. "You are sure you have told me all your bills?"

"Well – I owe fifty penceworth

of kindness to a little girl," said his sister in a feeble voice, and she told her brother about Mollie. "I don't know where she lives – so you can't very well pay her back."

"Well, I can pay it to someone else instead," said her brother. "If you owe someone fifty penceworth of kindness I must certainly deal with it!"

He watched for a chance, but it didn't come for some time. Then he saw a little girl knocked off her bicycle by a car, and he ran to pick her up. He put her in his own car, and took her to the nearest doctor. She wasn't very badly hurt, but she was very, very frightened.

The doctor soon bandaged her cut arm and leg, but Pamela still cried bitterly. "I'll take you home now," said Mrs Forrester's brother. "And on the way we'll stop at a toy shop, and I'll buy you a great big doll – but you must stop crying if I do that!"

"You're very kind!" said Pamela, shyly.

"Ah, I have a bit of kindness to pay to somebody," said Mrs Forrester's brother, and he told Pamela all about how kind Mollie had been to his sister and about the penny that George had given Mollie. "Well, here we are at the toy shop – and here's the very doll for you!"

He bought a beauty, and then drove Pamela home. He left her at the front door, and drove off, because he did not want to be thanked. Pamela went in and told her mother and father all that had happened. She showed them the beautiful doll.

"But who was this kind, generous fellow?" said her father. "Didn't you ask his name? I must find him and pay him back his great kindness to you."

But Pamela didn't know who had been so kind to her, and

looked after her and given her
the lovely doll. Her father tried
his hardest to find out, but he
couldn't.

Pamela was worried. "We
ought to pay back his kindness
somehow, Daddy, oughtn't we?"
she said. "It all began with that
pennyworth of kindness on the
bus – that kind man told me the
whole story – how a little boy
paid a penny for a little girl's
fare, and when she found she
couldn't pay it back, she bought
this man's sister fifty penceworth
of eggs, because hers got broken
– so that was fifty penceworth of
kindness – and the sister couldn't

pay it back because she didn't know where the little girl lived, so the brother said..."

"Said he'd pay it back, but to somebody else!" said her mother. she turned to Pamela's father. "John! A pennyworth of kindness became fifty penceworth. The fifty penceworth has become ten poundsworth, because that is exactly what the kind fellow paid for this doll!"

"And I shall make it a hundred poundsworth!" said Pamela's father. "My little girl is very precious to me, and I would give a hundred pounds to anyone in return for helping her. If only I could find this fellow."

But he couldn't. So do you know what he did? He spent his hundred pounds on buying new swings for the playground in the village, a new sand-pit for the children too, and he even put in a lovely paddling-pool for the little ones.

George goes there every Saturday, with his sister Jane and his little brother Ian. Ian plays in the sand-pit, Jane plays in the paddling-pool, George goes on the swings. They have a really wonderful time.

George doesn't know that all

these lovely playthings were put there because of his pennyworth of kindness. He just thinks that Pamela's father must be one of the kindest men in the world to give so many marvellous things to the children in the village.

How I'd love to give someone a pennyworth of kindness and see it grow and grow! Wouldn't you? Let's try it whenever we get the chance!

An Exciting
Afternoon

TOM was out on his bicycle one lovely afternoon. He was bird-watching!

He was very keen on nature, especially birds, and he knew more about them than anyone else at school. For his birthday his father had given him a wonderful present. It was a pair of binoculars!

He could see birds a long way away with them. It was such fun to sit down by a hedge, put his binoculars to his eyes, and watch a bird at the other end of the field. He could see what it did without frightening it at all.

Tom was sitting down,

perfectly quiet, his binoculars to his eyes, when somebody came along the road. Tom took no notice. He was watching a yellowhammer singing on the topmost branch of a bush a long way away.

The Somebody stopped when he saw Tom's bicycle propped against the hedge. He looked round cautiously. He could not see Tom on the other side. So, in a flash, the man took the bicycle, jumped on it, and pedalled off furiously down the lane!

Tom heard the noise and jumped up. He leaned over the gate by the hedge. His bicycle was gone – and there, away down the road, was a man riding it at top speed.

"Hey! Stop! That's my bike!" yelled Tom. But the man didn't stop, of course. He had a bag over his shoulder, and he pedalled along at about thirty miles an hour.

Tom was very angry. But what could he do? He could never catch the man up. Now he would have to walk home – and home was at least eight miles away. He had better start now, for it would take him ages.

"A lovely afternoon spoilt," said Tom, gloomily. He stepped

out down the lane, listening to another yellowhammer calling out something about bread and cheese.

Soon he came to the main road. After a bit a car came along. It was a police car! In the car were two burly policemen, whose keen eyes looked Tom up and down.

"What are you doing walking out here on your own?" asked the driver.

Tom went red. "I've had my bike stolen," he said. "And now I have to walk home."

"Oh! So you've had your bicycle stolen have you?" said

the second policeman. "I suppose you're some way from home, then?"

"About eight miles," said Tom.

"Then jump in and tell us about it," said the policeman. "We'll take you part of the way home, at any rate."

So Tom got in, feeling rather grand to be in a police car. The driver started up the engine and they shot off down the road.

Tom began to tell them about how his bicycle had been stolen. The car slid swiftly along as he told his tale.

And, just as Tom finished his story, he saw something that

made him sit up straight in the back of the car.

"Look! There's my bike! That must be the man who stole it, too, who's riding it now. I remember that he had a sack or something over his shoulder."

The policeman slowed down the car. "We'll ask him a few questions," said the driver, grimly. "Sure it's your bike, lad?"

"Oh, yes. I'd know it anywhere!" said Tom, in excitement. The police car shot by the man on the bicycle, came to a stop – and, just as the man reached the car, out jumped the two policemen!

The man almost fell off the bicycle with fright. One of the policemen caught the handlebars, and the man had to get off.

"Where did you get this bicycle?" asked the policeman.

"It's mine!" said the man. "Keep your hands off it. Let me go!" He tried to jump on and ride off, but he couldn't.

"Let's see what you've got in your sack," said the other policeman, and deftly took the sack from the man's shoulder. He opened it – and gave a loud exclamation.

"Whew! Look here!"

Tom and the other policeman looked. The sack was full of silver candlesticks, gold boxes and jewel cases.

"He's the fellow who has just robbed Lady Landley!" said the driver. "My word – we've only just got the message through – and we've got the thief! You'll have to come with us, man."

"Can I have my bicycle back?" asked Tom, eagerly.

"Oh, yes. He took it to make a quick getaway," said one of the policeman. "What a good thing you got a lift from us, sonny, and saw the fellow riding your bicycle. You get back your bike –

Lady Landley gets back her goods – and we get a very clever thief that we've been hunting for a very long while! A good afternoon's work!"

"It's been a most exciting afternoon!" said Tom. "And there's still time for me to go and do some bird-watching after all – but I think I really must go home and tell my mother and brother and sister what's happened. Good gracious – it's even more exciting than bird-watching!"

He rode off, and the policeman bundled the thief into the car, and drove him to a police-station. How surprised he was to be caught so quickly!

"How exciting!" thought Tom, as he pedalled quickly home. "Really, you never know what's going to happen!"